Oliver Orchid
meets
Dandy Lion

Written by Dr. Kendra Thornton

Illustrated by Chris Hilaire

Oliver Orchid Meets Dandy Lion

Copyright © 2020 Dr. Kendra Thornton

Produced and printed
by Stillwater River Publications.
All rights reserved. Written and produced in the
United States of America. This book may not be reproduced
or sold in any form without the expressed, written
permission of the author and publisher.

Visit our website at
www.StillwaterPress.com
for more information.

First Stillwater River Publications Edition

Library of Congress Control Number: 2020924960

ISBN: 978-1-955123-05-1

1 2 3 4 5 6 7 8 9 10
Written by Dr. Kendra Thornton
Illustrated by Chris Hilaire
Published by Stillwater River Publications,
Pawtucket, RI, USA.

Publisher's Cataloging-In-Publication Data
(Prepared by The Donohue Group, Inc.)

Names: Thornton, Kendra M., Dr., author. | Hilaire, Chris, illustrator.
Title: Oliver Orchid meets Dandy Lion / written by Dr. Kendra M. Thornton ;
illustrated by Chris Hilaire.
Description: First Stillwater River Publications edition. | Pawtucket, RI, USA :
Stillwater River Publications, [2021] | Interest age level: 004-009. |
Summary: "Oliver Orchid is an anxious kitty whose fears cause him to miss out on
fun adventures. When Oliver Orchid meets a resilient cub, Dandy Lion, he learns
from their friendship that he must strengthen his 'brave muscles' and move
through his anxiety"--Provided by publisher.
Identifiers: ISBN 9781952521409
Subjects: LCSH: Cats--Juvenile fiction. | Lion--Juvenile fiction. |
Courage--Juvenile fiction. | Anxiety--Juvenile fiction. | CYAC: Cats--Fiction. |
Lion--Fiction. | Courage--Fiction. | Anxiety--Fiction.
Classification: LCC PZ7.1.T516 O45 2021 | DDC [E]--dc23

For my husband Rob and our Ollie,

who inspired this book.

Meet Oliver Orchid. He is a very fussy kitty. Not fuzzy *(though he is that too)* but fussy! Everything has to be just right for him to feel safe and happy.

Oliver Orchid will only eat one type
of tuna fish from his favorite red bowl.
Tuna in a blue bowl?
Nope!
Tuna on a yellow plate?
No way!
Oliver Orchid would rather go hungry.

Oliver Orchid will only go to sleep when he has his special purple blanket and his star nightlight.
If the blanket is in the laundry or his nightlight burns out, he will simply refuse to close his eyes.

Oliver Orchid is a funny and smart kitty who loves to play with other animals, *but...* they must play *his* games and follow *his rules*.

He is a kind kitty and wants to be a good friend, but it's difficult for Oliver Orchid to compromise.

He doesn't do this to be unkind. He does it because being in control makes him feel safe. When things don't go his way, he might cry, but he is not sad. He may yell, but he is not mad. Oliver Orchid feels very, **very, very** scared.

When Oliver Orchid feels things spin out of his control, he becomes an anxious kitty.

Sometimes Oliver Orchid's anxiety is so strong that he feels changes in his body. He will get a tummyache and his face will feel hot. On anxious days, doing the things he loves to do feels very difficult. His worries keep him from enjoying the good things around him.

One day, Oliver Orchid sees another kitty playing in the forest. He watches her climb the tallest trees and walk along the branches. When the kitty falls off the tree limb, she simply dusts off her paws, hops back up, and starts climbing again. Oliver is amazed by this brave bouncing kitty who isn't scared of heights. He admires how she keeps climbing the trees even after falling out of them. Oliver is inspired to learn more about this new kitty, but he isn't sure what to say to her.

The other kitty sees Oliver Orchid and
skips over to greet him.

"Hi, I'm Dandy Lion!" she says with a smile.
"My mom says I'm like a dandelion because
I can grow strong and be okay anywhere I go.
Do you want to climb trees together?"

"Hi Dandy Lion, I'm Oliver Orchid.
I'm scared to climb trees. It looks like so much fun,
but the trees are tall and I could fall down."

Oliver Orchid watches Dandy Lion bounce back over to the tree and hop from branch to branch. "Isn't that hard to do?" Oliver asks.

Dandy replies, "Yes, but I can do a lot of difficult things. My SUPERPOWER is that I always try! When I climbed my first tree I was scared too, but I decided it is more fun to try something new and fail than not try at all. Nobody is great at everything right away. We all need practice to get better."

"But aren't you scared?" Oliver replies cautiously.

"Nope," says Dandy confidently. "When I fail at something new, it makes my 'brave muscles' grow stronger. I'm not the fastest lion or the strongest lion, but I can be the lion that tries the hardest. Do you know what I learned, Oliver?"

"What?" Oliver asks, eager for the answer.

"If I don't give up, then I grow stronger and faster because I tried something new. When I face a big challenge, I don't see it as a hurdle. Instead, I see challenges as building blocks!" states Dandy Lion confidently.

Oliver had to agree, it seemed like a better idea to try to climb the trees than to miss out on all the fun.

The two kitties spent the rest of the day

playing and laughing in the treetops.

Oliver felt himself grow braver with every

pounce and bounce!

Over time, Oliver became less scared. He was better able to handle it when things didn't go the way he wanted at home and he worried less about new challenges at school.

Life wasn't always easy, but Oliver
knew he was brave enough to try.
He became less and less fussy, *but*...

Oliver Orchid stayed extra FUZZY
and that felt just right to him!

For Parents, Caregivers, and Educators

DISCUSSION QUESTIONS

1. Oliver Orchid is described as an anxious kitty. Describe what you think it means to be anxious.

2. Oliver found it difficult to compromise. Why is it important to learn to compromise with friends?

3. What types of things did Oliver Orchid need to have to feel safe?

4. Tell me about a time you felt worried.

5. Sometimes we feel our feelings in our bodies. Maybe your face feels hot when you are angry or your belly feels funny when you are excited. What changes do you notice in your body when you are scared?

6. What are some ways you can calm yourself down when you feel upset?

7. What types of things did Dandy Lion do that made her brave?

8. Tell me about a time you felt brave.

9. How did Dandy Lion help Oliver Orchid be less scared about new things?

10. Tell me about a time you tried something new and what you learned.

About the Author

After many years collaborating with families as a mental health therapist, school counselor, and principal, Dr. Kendra Thornton was eager to convert resilience research into her first children's book. She earned her doctorate, with a specialization in neuroeducation, at Johns Hopkins University. Dr. Thornton is passionate about a holistic approach to education that emphasizes mental health and social-emotional wellness.

About the Illustrator

Chris Hilaire is a Haitian-American artist born in New York. Ever since he first read *The Edge Chronicles* he knew he wanted to be an Illustrator. Particularly interested in painting worlds of fantasy, he chooses bright colors that can easily spark anyone's imagination. As a freelance Illustrator, he especially enjoys creating images for book projects that captivate his younger self, taking viewers along a visual journey, while filling them with reminiscent joy that will stay with them in the future.

Lightning Source UK Ltd.
Milton Keynes UK
UKHW050500270521
384314UK00008B/26